FLY GUY AND THE FRANKENFLY

Tedd Arnold

CARTWHEEL BOOKS

An Imprint of Scholastic Inc.

Specially for Owen and Kei!

ISBN 978-0-545-79354-4

Copyright © 2013 by Tedd Arnold. All rights reserved. Published by Scholastic Inc. SCHOLASTIC, CARTWHEEL BOOKS, and associated logos are trademarks and/or registered trademarks of Scholastic Inc.

12 11 10 9 8 7 6 5 4 3 2   17 18 19/0

Printed in the U.S.A.   40

First Scholastic paperback printing, October 2014

A boy had a pet fly.
He named him Fly Guy.
And Fly Guy could
say the boy's name—

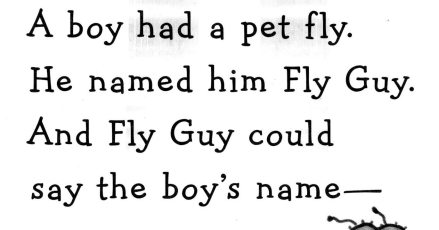

BUZZ!

Chapter 1

It was a dark and stormy night. Buzz and Fly Guy were playing.

Buzz made puzzles
for both of them.

Buzz made costumes
for both of them.

Buzz made a drawing
for both of them.

Finally, Buzz said,
"Time for bed, Fly Guy."

Fly Guy said,

BIZZY!

As Buzz fell asleep,
he wondered, "What
is Fly Guy making?"

Chapter 2

Late that night a strange light woke up Buzz.

Fly Guy was making
something in his laboratory.

He was making a monster!

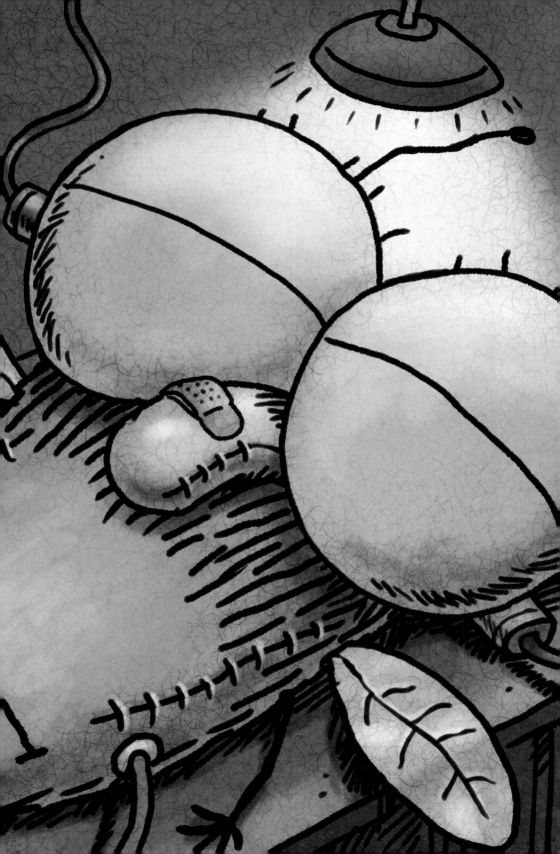

Fly Guy turned on the power.

The monster sat up.

Buzz cried, "It's Frankenfly!"

Frankenfly heard Buzz.
He stood up.

He walked to the bed.

17

Frankenfly picked up Buzz.

Fly Guy yelled,

Fly Guy shut off the power.

CRASH!

Frankenfly dropped Buzz
and fell onto the bed.

Chapter 3

Buzz fell out of bed and woke up. It was morning.

CRASH!

"Wow!" said Buzz. "That was a *bad* dream."

Fly Guy was not in his bed.

He was asleep on the desk.

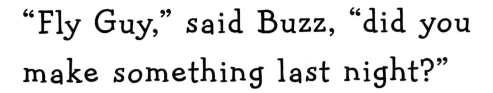

"Fly Guy," said Buzz, "did you make something last night?"

Fly Guy said,

"You made me?" asked Buzz.

"YEZZZ!" said Fly Guy.

He pointed to a piece of paper.

"It's me!" said Buzz.

"It's a painting of you and me!" said Buzz.

"How did you paint this? My brushes are too big for you."

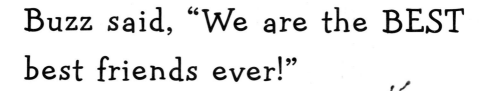

Buzz said, "We are the BEST best friends ever!"